Where Will My Shoes Take Me?

By Deb Manikas • Illustrated by Robin Boyer

Outskirts Press, Inc.
http://www.outskirtspress.com

Paperback ISBN: 978-1-9772-3118-5
Hardback ISBN: 978-1-9772-3601-2

Illustrations by: Robin Boyer. All rights reserved - used with permission.

Outskirts Press and the "OP" logo are trademarks belonging to Outskirts Press, Inc.

PRINTED IN THE UNITED STATES OF AMERICA

For my five children,
my life's greatest blessings
and to my grandchildren,
my greatest joys.

A special thank you to
my Dad and my sisters,
for always believing in me.

This Book Belongs to:

_____

Every morning I put on my shoes.
Sometimes I wear BIG shoes.

My shoes fit me just right today.
Shoes take me on adventures!

Where will my pirate shoes take me today?

My shoes take me to build a fort
and find treasure.

Where will my mud shoes take me today?

My shoes take me to jump in the pond and hunt for turtles and frogs.

Look at these funny shoes.
Where will my shoes take me today?

My shoes take me to make a snowman!

I am wearing these work shoes today.
Where will my shoes take me?

My shoes take me to dig a big hole.

Look at these water shoes.
Where will my shoes take me today?

My shoes take me to build sandcastles and dig for shells on the beach.

Where will my party shoes take me today?

My shoes take me to
Grandma's birthday party!

These are summer shoes.
Where will my shoes take me?

My shoes take me to a picnic in the park with my family today.

Sometimes I take my shoes off.
Where will my bare feet take
me today?

They take me to splash in mud puddles!

Look at these big shoes.
Where will my shoes take me someday?

My shoes take me to be a BIG kid soon!

Look at these fuzzy shoes.
Where will they take me tonight?

For now, my shoes will take me HOME!

the end

CPSIA information can be obtained
at www.ICGtesting.com
Printed in the USA
BVHW021311201220
595735BV00004B/81